D1552925

PATIENCE LARGE PRINT

AMISH ROMANCE

RUTH HARTZLER

Amish
ROMANCE BOOKS

Patience Large Print
Amish Romance
(The Amish Buggy Horse, Book 4)
Ruth Hartzler
Copyright © 2015 Ruth Hartzler
All Rights Reserved
ISBN 9781925689310

This is a work of fiction. Any resemblance to any person, living or dead, is purely coincidental. The personal names have been invented by the author, and any likeness to the name of any person, living or dead, is purely coincidental.

GLOSSARY

Pennsylvania Dutch is a dialect, not a language, because it has no standard written form. It is written as it sounds, which is why you will see the same word written several different ways. All are permissible.

The word 'Dutch' has nothing to do with Holland, but rather is likely a corruption of the German word 'Deitsch' or 'Deutsch'.

ab im kopp - addled in the head

Ach! (also, *Ack!*) - Oh!

aenti - aunt

appeditlich - delicious

Ausbund - Amish hymn book

bedauerlich - sad

bloobier - blueberry

boppli - baby

bopplin - babies

bro - bread

bruder(s) - brother(s)

bu - boy

Budget, The - weekly newspaper for Amish and Mennonite communities. Based on Sugarcreek, Ohio, and has 2 versions, Local and National.

buwe - boys

daag - day

Daed, Datt, Dat (vocative) - Dad

Diary, The - Lancaster County based Amish newspaper. Focus is on Old Order Amish.

Dawdi (also, *Daadi*) (vocative) - Grandfather

dawdi haus (also, *daadi haus, grossdawdi haus*) - grandfather's or grandparents' house (often a small house behind the main house)

de Bo - boyfriend

Die Botschaft - Amish weekly newspaper. Based in PA but its focus is nation-wide.

demut - humility

denki (or *danki*) - thank you

Der Herr - The Lord

dochder - daughter

dokter - doctor

doplich - clumsy

dumm - dumb

dummkopf - idiot, dummy

Dutch Blitz - Amish card game

English (or *Englisch*) (adjective) - A non-Amish person

Englischer (noun) - A non-Amish person

familye - family

ferhoodled - foolish, crazy

fraa - wife, woman

froh - happy

freind - friend

freinden - friends

gegisch - silly

geh - go

gern gheschen (also, gern *gschehne*) - you're welcome

Gott (also, *Gotte*) - God

grank - sick, ill

grossboppli - grandbaby

grossdawdi (also, *dawdi, daadi haus, gross dawdi*) - grandfather, or, in some communities, great grandfather

grosskinskind - great-grandchild

grosskinskinner - great-grandchildren

grossmammi (or *grossmudder*) - grandmother

gross-sohn - grandson

grossvadder - grandfather (see also *grossdawdi*)

gude mariye - good morning

guten nacht (also, *gut nacht*) - good night

gude nochmiddaag - good afternoon

gut - good

haus - house

Herr - Mr.

Hiya - Hi

hochmut - pride

Hullo (also, *Hallo*) - Hello

hungerich - hungry

Ich liebe dich - I love you

jah (also *ya*) - yes

kaffi (also, *kaffee*) - coffee

kapp - prayer covering worn by women

kichli - cookie

kichlin - cookies

kinn (also, *kind*) - child

kinner - children

kinskinner - Grandchildren

Kumme (or *Kumm*) - Come

lieb - love, sweetheart

liewe - a term of endearment, dear, love

liede - song

maid (also, *maed*) - girls

maidel (also, *maedel*) - girl

Mamm (also, *Mammi*) - Mother, Mom

Mammi - Grandmother

mann - man

mariye-esse - breakfast

mei - my

meidung - shunning

mei lieb - my love

mein liewe - my dear, my love

menner - men

mudder - mother

naerfich - nervous

naut (also, *nacht*) - night

nee (also *nein*) - no

nix - nothing

nohma - name

onkel - uncle

Ordnung - "Order", the unwritten Amish set of rules, different in each community

piffle (also, *piddle*) - to waste time or kill time

Plain - referring to the Amish way of life

rett (also, *redd*) - to put (items) away or to clean up.

rootsh (also, *ruch*) - not being able to sit still.

rumspringa (also, *rumschpringe*) - Running around years - when Amish youth (usually around the age of sixteen) leave the community for time and can be English, and decide whether to commit to the Amish way of life and be baptized.

schatzi - honey

schee - pretty, handsome

schecklich - scary

schmaert - smart

schtupp - family room

schweschder - sister

schweschdern - sisters

schwoger - brother-in-law

seltsam - strange, unnatural

sohn - son

vadder - father

verboten - forbidden

Vorsinger - Song leader

was its let - what is the matter?

wie gehts - how are you?

wilkum (also, *wilkom*) - welcome

wunderbar (also, *wunderbaar*) - wonderful

yer - you

yourself - yourself

youngie (also, *young)* - the youth

yung - young

CHAPTER 1

From the comfort of her warm bed, Patience could see the snow flakes swirling outside. Animals were waiting to be fed, but the bed was so cozy and warm; surely the animals could wait a few more minutes.

Patience watched the snow falling in soft and fluffy waves. Ice crystals were forming on the edges of the window. "Simon," she sighed aloud. He was so sweet and thoughtful, not to mention handsome. Patience wanted to drift back to sleep and dream about all the possibilities before her, the possibilities of her future with Simon.

At that point, Patience's *mudder* poked her head around the door. "Patience, just because you're on *rumspringa* doesn't mean you can escape doing your chores."

Patience sighed. "Sorry, *Mamm*. I'm getting up now."

"And make sure you brush your hair."

"*Jah*." Patience lay in bed a little longer, continuing her thoughts of Simon. Simon was six feet tall with broad shoulders and kind eyes. His wild blonde hair fell into his eyes most of the time, hiding the mischief that Patience was sure was hidden in them. Patience, on the other hand, was only a little over five feet tall. Her *mudder* always said that Patience could disappear into a snow drift and never be found.

Patience sighed and went down to the

kitchen, where her *mudder* had a steaming mug of *kaffi* waiting for her. After *kaffi* and a big breakfast of scrapple and cereal topped with fruit, Patience hurried outside to do her chores, with Simon still on her mind.

Later, as Patience drove the old truck to Simon's *familye's haus*, the smile stayed on her face. Even before she put her truck in park, he was hurrying her way.

Simon jumped in the passenger seat and tossed the biscuits onto the dash. He leaned over to her. "It's about time! I was freezing out here."

Patience smiled and waved the thermos in his handsome face. "I brought *kaffi*."

Simon reached into his coat and pulled out a jar of his *mudder's* raspberry jam. He opened the jar and handed it over with a biscuit. Soon the mugs were filled, and they happily enjoyed their simple breakfast.

"Are you still going to leave me?"

Patience's heart wrenched when she heard the sadness in his voice. She ate a glob of jam off her thumb and sighed. "I'm not leaving you. I'm going on vacation with my *familye* in Florida for the holidays. This year's like every other year; I'll be back before you know it." Patience stole a glance at Simon to see if he was upset.

"I don't know what I'm going to do while you're gone," he lamented. "There's not going to be any *kaffi* in the morning, and I'll have to eat all the extra food my *mudder* makes for you until you get back. I'll probably look like a fat, old *mann* by then." Simon pouted and stuck out his bottom lip for the full effect.

Patience laughed. "I'll be back before you know it."

CHAPTER 2

"Patience, I'll finish up here if you want to say goodbye to Simon. His *mudder* tells me he's at the Farm Hill café this morning."

"*Denki, Mamm.*" Without a further thought, Patience raced for the old truck.

Her feet flew down the stairs and barely stopped long enough to snatch her coat. Before she could even get her arms in the sleeves, she put the key in the ignition.

Patience reached the Farm Hill café, after

carefully driving through town. She was glad she was allowed to drive the old, borrowed truck; not all her friends' parents had allowed them to drive when on *rumspringa*. Where was Simon? She lifted up off the seat and tried to gain an extra couple of inches to look out the windshield. Finally, there it was; the old blue car Simon was driving while on *rumspringa*.

She searched the area around his truck and spotted him at once. Every time she saw him, it took her breath away. Today he was bundled in a thick, hooded sweatshirt with a black down vest and jeans. His cheeks were bright red from the cold and wind. Even this early in the day, the skies were dark. Just as she was about to honk and get his attention, someone ran up behind him.

Patience's truck slowed down almost to a halt when she saw the scene before her. Her best friend Waneta ran up beside Simon and slipped her arm through his. With his hood on, it was hard to see Simon's face, but it didn't matter. Patience's stomach was suddenly queasy. Why was Waneta with Simon? And why hadn't Waneta told her that she would be in town that day?

Patience wanted to jump out of her truck and run to him, but fear held her in place. She watched them walk, arm in arm, toward Simon's truck. Instead of Waneta walking away, Simon opened the passenger door for her and shut her inside.

Simon ran around and climbed inside. In the blink of an eye they were gone. Patience's hands grasped the steering wheel as she sat there in shock. A horn blared behind her and snapped her out of her trance. She pulled into the first empty spot she could find, trying to field off a panic attack.

Yet surely there was nothing to be worried about? Simon was a generous and kind *mann* - and trustworthy. There had to be a good excuse for him driving Waneta around. That was it; there was an explanation, and Patience was going to go and get it.

Patience pried her fingers off the steering wheel and found her cell phone. It took a couple of tries, but she finally managed to call Simon's number. She tried to calm her breathing while it rang, hoping she would sound happy and light when he answered.

Yet he did not answer. The call went through to Simon's voicemail. "*Hullo, hullo*, Simon," she stammered. "I found some time to get away and see you. I guess you're busy. I'll talk to you later."

Patience drove around for a while, hoping he would call back while she was still in the truck. While her parents permitted her to have the cell phone while on *rumspringa*, they did not allow her to use it inside their *haus*.

Finally, Patience gave up and pointed the truck back in the direction of her home. There was still no word from Simon, so she drove to the pond and watched the snow falling softly onto the bare limbs of the hackberry trees. Patience was just about to drive back when he called. She didn't want to appear to be jealous, but told him that she had seen Waneta getting into his car with him.

Simon laughed it away. "Waneta had car trouble and asked me to drive her back and take a look at the engine. When I fixed it, she was so happy that she insisted on buying me dinner. We had wings at the Farm Hill café."

Patience let out a long sigh of relief. She didn't want to be jealous. She was leaving the following morning, and, despite being on *rumspringa*, her parents wanted her to dress Amish while on vacation and to leave the cell phone behind.

When they arrived back home a few days earlier than planned, Patience hurried as fast as she could to Simon's *haus*. Mrs. Warner opened the door as soon as she knocked.

"Patience, you're back."

"*Hullo*, Mrs. Warner. I was wondering if Simon..."

Mrs. Warner laughed, a soft and warm laugh. "Simon and some friends are down at Farm Hill café. He'll be so pleased to see you."

Patience drove carefully toward the busy downtown area to Farm Hill café, an old café that served mainly locals, unlike the popular and loud café across the road. She drove past the small building and looked for parking. Between the snow drifts and the crowd, there wasn't a space to be found. She circled around again and hoped that something had opened up. With no luck there, she drove further down and found a spot about three blocks away.

The icy wind hit her in the face the minute

she opened her door. Patience pulled her coat tightly around her, and pushed forward toward Farm Hill café, smiling in anticipation at seeing Simon. She stopped at the corner and looked both ways to cross.

That's when she saw them, Waneta with Simon. Simon was laughing, presumably at something Waneta had said. He looked happy.

Patience was unable to move; she was frozen in place, stunned by what she was seeing.

Simon wrapped his arm around Waneta's shoulder and led her into Farm Hill café.

Patience stood there, dumbstruck. She could not figure out what to do. There was no reason she could conceive that made sense for them being together.

Patience forced herself to walk into the café. She stayed by the entrance and scanned the room. By the back, in a large booth, were

Simon and Waneta. They were laughing and talking.

Patience walked back to the truck with the sight burned in her mind. What should she do now? She did not want to go back home; her stomach was churning and she felt physically ill. Perhaps there was an innocent reason why Simon and Waneta were together? Patience did not want to do anything impulsive, so sat in the truck, her fingers gripping the wheel until her knuckles turned white.

Finally she could not stand it any longer, so headed back out into the ice and snow. Patience wandered aimlessly until she found herself at the local bakery. Surely a buttery croissant would make her feel better.

Her head still drifted in endless questions, so much so, that she almost missed Waneta sitting with two *Englischer* girls at a table by the front window. The trio stopped talking the minute that Patience stepped inside.

"Patience!" Waneta waved her hand in the air at Patience.

Patience hesitated. She did not want to talk to Waneta, but perhaps she would get the answers she needed. *"Hullo."* Patience forced a smile to her face and held up a finger to ask for a minute while she ordered.

When Patience walked to Waneta's table, she noted that Waneta appeared nervous; she continually glanced at the other girls at the table. *"Hiya,* Patience. I thought you were still on vacation. What on earth are you doing here?" Waneta's voice was high pitched and edgy, as if she were guilty.

Patience's appetite had deserted her, but she had ordered a croissant and a jumbo coffee anyway. *"Jah,* that was the plan, but my *vadder* wanted to come back a little early. Anyway, I missed Simon." Patience watched Waneta's face as she said the words.

Patience judged that Waneta appeared

surprised, but hid it almost instantly. Waneta raised her coffee cup to her lips and took a sip. "Have you seen him yet, Patience? I mean, when did you get in?" Waneta giggled, with her hand in front of her mouth.

Despite the fact that it was none of Waneta's business, Patience answered truthfully. "I've just got back. I went to his *mudder's haus* and she said that Simon was at Farm Hill café with friends. Did you all have a good time?"

Patience saw the change in Waneta's expression, and at once, she wanted to run away. She did not want to know what Waneta was going to say, as she sensed it was not going to be good.

Waneta cast her eyes downwards in a coy gesture. "Patience, um, this isn't how I wanted you to find out. Simon should have told you by now. It's nothing personal. It just sort of happened." She looked at the other girls from under her lashes.

Patience tightened her grip on her cup. "What? What just happened? Waneta, I don't understand what you're saying."

The two *Englischer* girls stopped giggling when Waneta spoke again. "I'm sorry, Patience. We're together; Simon and I are dating. It's gotten serious quickly, and we've been to the bishop. Simon didn't know how to tell you. It started just before you went away. I'm so sorry, Patience."

Her words fell away as Patience stood and hurried away. She could not hear any more. Her head pounded and her stomach churned. Tears burned at the back of her eyes.

Patience hurried to her truck, almost slipping on a patch of ice. Her coffee flew out of her hands, and landed in a dark pool on the snow. She jumped in her truck.

Patience drove away in a hurry. She just drove; her heart was so broken. Flurries fell again.

Like her hurt and pain, they came faster with time. She did not slow down.

As Patience pulled onto the road that led to her *haus*, she skid on a patch of ice, but managed to right the car. Tears were falling freely, blurring the scene before her into one big mess of white. At that moment, her phone rang.

Crying, Patience clutched at the phone beside her. It was likely Simon, and she wanted to toss the phone out the window. With only one hand on the wheel, she was unable to steady the car when she hit another patch of ice. The tires slid to the right, taking her straight into a utility pole.

I shouldn't have been going that fast, Patience thought as she spun in what seemed like slow motion. *I shouldn't have loved him so much. I shouldn't have gone for a croissant.*

Then her vision went dark and the sound of crushing metal filled the air.

CHAPTER 3

One minute Patience was driving, and the next minute, all went dark. She lay in the darkness for what seemed like forever. There were people around her, but she could not see them. She thought they were talking to her, but she wasn't sure. All she knew for sure was that she was tired. Her body felt so heavy.

The next thing that Patience remembered was an annoying beeping sound that would not stop. She tried to open her eyes, but they felt too heavy. Patience fought against rising panic; something was wrong. She did not like the way she felt. Patience opened her mouth in an attempt to speak, but her throat felt like sandpaper. Instead of a voice, the sound that came out of her mouth was a low growl.

Patience tried to move her body, but it wasn't cooperating with her. It was then that she became aware that someone was holding her hand. Whoever it was tightened their grip on her when she made the sound. Patience blinked wildly, and in what seemed to her like slow motion, opened her eyes.

She at once regretted doing so. The light was so bright that it made everything worse. Patience's *vadder's* face slowly came into view. *Datt looks worried*, she thought. *Why is he so worried?*

Patience tried to speak again, but it was useless. She was mute for the moment. She saw her *mudder* standing next to her *vadder*. Why were they so upset?

Patience's *mudder* bent over her. "You lost control of the truck on a patch of ice. It was really coming down when they finally found you. There was at least two feet of snow packed around your truck."

Patience's *mudder* kept explaining, but Patience was unable to take it all in. Finally, the doctor came in and sent everyone away. He explained that Patience had broken her left arm at the elbow, that she needed minor surgery to insert a pin. Patience also had stitches on her head, face and arm, as well as a serious concussion and bruised ribs in the mix. "Are you in much pain?" he concluded.

Patience tried to nod, but that hurt, so instead she croaked, "Yes." There wasn't an inch of her that didn't hurt. It seemed to her that even her eyelashes hurt.

The doctor informed Patience that she was staying put for at least a couple of weeks, and explained to her about the pain medication, but Patience was unable to take it all in.

When he left, an efficient nurse bustled in and deposited some Jell-O and tea next to the bed, and then left just as abruptly. Patience huddled in the itchy hospital sheets and tried to go back to sleep to make the pain go away.

When she awoke sometime later, Simon was there.

The sight of him brought it all back. He was the last person she wanted to see. There was no way she was ready to deal with this yet; she wanted him gone.

Simon hurried over to her bed. "You scared me so much. I was the one who found your truck. There was so much snow, and I couldn't get in fast enough." Simon's words tumbled out one after the other, all in a rush. His face was white and drawn.

For a second Patience wanted to hold him, to

comfort him and ease his discomfort. Yet that was just for a second, for she had nothing to say. In fact, she felt that she would never have anything to say to him again. Her heart and body were equally broken. Simon needed to disappear from her sight, and disappear right now.

"Patience, please talk to me. I almost lost you yesterday. Please talk to me. I don't understand what's going on." His voice cracked with emotion. "You were supposed to be in Florida. I was driving by, and I saw a truck buried in the snow. The closer I got," - he swallowed hard - "I realized it was your truck." Simon stopped for a minute before continuing. "At first I thought someone had tried to steal your truck, but then I saw your hair through the back window. I, I," he stammered.

Patience had no tolerance or sympathy for Simon. All she wanted him to do was to stop talking. *If Simon feels guilty and needs sympathy, well he won't find it here*, she thought. *If that's what he wants, he can go and see Waneta.* "Get out," she said aloud.

Patience saw his surprise. "Get out." She repeated the order with as much force as she could muster.

Simon's face turned even whiter. "You don't mean that, Patience. I love you. Please talk to me. What's going on? I don't understand anything that's happening here." He moved closer to her face. His hand reached out and stroked her cheek.

Patience flinched at his touch. It was all a lie. He had lied to her, and his tender concern now was clearly simply his guilt surfacing, and nothing more. Well, it most certainly was not her job to make him feel better.

"Get out. Go find Waneta." She forced the words out of her mouth.

Patience watched as Simon's mouth opened

and close like a fish. He stepped back and paced around the room.

"What does Waneta have to do with this? Patience, what is going on with you?" He spread his arms wide.

Patience's anger provided her with a boost of adrenaline. She pushed herself up as far as she could with one arm. "Please go away; I never want to see you again."

Patience's *mudder* and *vadder* came back in at that point, but Patience doubted that they had heard her words. Simon hesitated for a moment, looked at everyone, and then hurried out of the room.

Patience should have been pleased to be released from the hospital, but coming home simply reminded her of Simon. She was unable to tell her *mudder* what had happened.

"Patience, it's natural to feel upset after what happened to you," her *mudder* said. "Time is all you need to feel better. It's normal to feel lost and afraid. You just have to give it time."

Time was not the answer. There was never going to be enough time to mend this hurt. "*Nee, nee, Mamm*. I'm sorry, but that's not enough. I need to go. Please let me go. I can go and stay with *Aenti* Carrie in Ohio, at least until I get over it all. She could use the company."

As Patience spoke, tears overwhelmed her. Through the veil of her tears, she could see that her *mudder* was trying to console her, to no avail.

"And *Mamm*, I don't ever want to hear about Simon. Please don't write to me about him. Whatever happens, I don't want to hear anything about him, nothing at all. Patience looked up into her *mudder's* confused face. "Promise me, *Mamm*?"

A week later, Patience was on the bus to her *ant's haus* in Ohio. She kept her eyes trained out the window. She was serious about a new life. The past was where it belonged - in the past. She just wanted to forget about it all.

For months, Patience had trouble sleeping at night. She would lay awake wondering what went wrong. Then she wondered where Simon was and what he was doing. It was an endless spiral of unanswered questions. Yet, unlike the pain of her broken arm, the pain of her broken heart dulled over time, but never disappeared altogether.

CHAPTER 4

SIX YEARS LATER

"How bad is it, *Mamm*? Why did this happen?" Patience gripped the phone tightly and looked up into *Aenti* Carrie's concerned face. Everything was out of control, and her head was spinning.

"The doctors don't know; they're running some tests." Patience heard her *mudder's* voice break over *Aenti* Carrie's barn phone.

"Of course I'll come home, *Mamm*. I'll come as fast as I can."

And so, only days later, Patience lay in the dark of her old bedroom listening to the old, familiar sounds, and chastising herself for being away from home for so long. How had it come to this? Why had she stayed away for years, when her initial intent had been only to stay with her *Aenti* Carrie for a few months? There was only one answer. It was a name that she had tried to push from her mind for six years, but one she still heard in her dreams. Simon Warner.

Still, there was no time to ponder lost love, as the next few days left her no time to worry about anything other than her *vadder*. Between long trips to the hospital and her *vadder's* harness making and repair shop, Patience was exhausted by the flurry of activity.

That night, Patience was unable to sleep, so went down to the kitchen where she found her *mudder* sitting at the old, wooden kitchen table, her head in her hands. "I can't sleep without all his snoring," her *mudder* said in a quiet voice. "After all these years, it's just too quiet."

Her *mudder* poured Patience a cup of tea and put out some scrapple, a mixture of cornmeal and meat. "He won't be able to handle the business like before. It's too much work, too much stress," she said to herself as much as to Patience. "Jake's a *gut mann* but he can't take on all your *vadder's* work as well at the buggy shop."

Patience nodded. She realized that there was no way that her *vadder* could keep up his busy harness making and repair business now without her help. Guilt washed over her again and again. "*Mamm*, I'm so sorry I stayed away for so long."

Her *mudder* tried to push her concerns aside with a wave of her hand. "You wrote every week."

Patience shook her head. "That's no excuse

for not coming back. I don't know why I stayed away so long. *Aenti* Carrie needed help at first, but now her *kinskinner* are old enough to help her with the chores. I," she hesitated, "kind of just fell into it, I suppose."

Her mother put her head down again. "The problem now is the business. Jake can do the labor but you will need to handle the finances. You said that *Aenti* Carrie trained you in helping with the accounts in her fabric store."

It was more of a statement than a question, but Patience nodded. Her heart sank, and she groaned inwardly. Of course she was home to stay; why hadn't she realized that? There was no fleeing to *Aenti* Carrie's now. She was home for good. How would she do it? She would run into Simon sooner or later.

Her *mudder* appeared to have guessed her thoughts. "You can't run forever, Patience. The past is just that. And, *jah*, it is inevitable that you will run into Simon at some point in time, at the next church meeting, if not sooner. You said that your leaving was your chance for a new life, a fresh start. But all you've done is let him take away any chance at a future you might have had."

Patience shook her head. She didn't want to know. She didn't care to know anything about Simon Warner. Her *mudder* on the other hand had a different idea. "Simon waited for you. I think he really believed you'd come back. When you didn't, he moved on. I didn't blame him. He married Waneta." Her mother fixed her eyes on Patience. "But Simon wasn't the same *mann* he used to be."

Patience was unable to stop the tears that fell from her eyes. Her heart was broken. Simon and Waneta, married. She had assumed that would be the case, but to hear it said aloud was quite another matter. Even after all this time had passed, Simon still had the power to hurt her immeasurably.

Her *mudder* was still talking. "They were married three years, but Waneta died from complications when having her second *boppli*."

Patience gasped. Waneta was gone? She had died? All these years she had disliked Waneta and now she was gone. "Why didn't you tell me?" Her voice came out as nothing more than a whisper.

"You didn't want to know. You made us promise never to say a word about Simon or anything to do with him. How could I tell you? You shut down the minute we even got close to mentioning Simon. Waneta went to be with *Gott* and left Simon to raise two little girls. Patience, he's been alone since the day you tossed him out of the hospital."

Simon, alone, raising two *dochders*? Patience had never told her *mudder* that Simon had been dating Waneta behind her back. Her *mudder* didn't have the full picture. Of course, her *mudder* would think that Simon had wanted her, when it had been Waneta whom he had wanted all the time. Still, Patience was unable to process all this information. All she knew, was that she was stuck in town for the foreseeable future. Like it or not, she still missed Simon. Even after all these years, she still missed everything about him.

"Why does it have to hurt so much?" Patience looked at her *mudder*. "I don't know what to do."

Her *mudder's* response was decidedly practical, as usual. "First, you will take over the accounts at your *vadder's* shop. Before that, you will climb into bed and try to get a decent night's sleep. But, Patience, you are going to have to find a way to prepare yourself to see Simon."

CHAPTER 5

Patience did not, in fact, have a good night's sleep. Simon was a father? She was unable to imagine that. What did they look like? Two little girls.

That morning, Patience's head was still in a fog as she rode to the hospital with her *mudder* in a taxi. Her *mudder* was excited as the doctors had said that Mr. Beiler might be released that day.

When they reached Mr. Beiler's room, a kindly nurse informed them that the doctors were with him now, and suggested they return in thirty or so minutes.

"Will he be discharged today?" Mrs. Beiler asked the nurse.

"That's no doubt what the doctors are deciding now."

Mrs. Beiler thanked the nurse and then turned to Patience. "Come on; there's a cafeteria on the ground floor of the hospital. It's near the emergency department entrance. We can wait there."

Patience wasn't hungry, despite the fact that they had left before breakfast. It had been a long drive to the hospital. She was concerned for her *mudder*, however, as she was looking white and drawn. No doubt her *mudder* was worried as to whether or not Mr. Beiler was about to be discharged. Patience decided to select something to eat in order to encourage her *mudder* to eat too.

"What are you having, *Mamm*?"

Her *mudder* shook her head. "*Nee*, Patience, I'm not hungry. You get something. I'll just have *kaffi*."

It was Patience's turn to shake her head. "*Nee, Mamm*. I won't eat unless you do. Come on, we both should eat something to keep up our strength in case *Daed* is discharged today. It's a long way home, and we'll be faint if we don't eat. Would you like an omelet? Or what about some hard fried eggs?"

"I suppose I could have a sandwich. I don't care what it is; you choose, Patience."

It was already busy, but two people vacated a table right by the window, overlooking the street. Patience's *mudder* at once sat down, while Patience went to buy their food.

Patience soon returned to the table with two sandwiches, a cup of coffee with steamed milk for herself and a cappuccino for her *mudder*.

"Here, *Mamm*, I got two different sandwiches, so you choose one and I'll have the other. This one is grilled chicken with red peppers, tomato, and pesto, and this one is turkey apple; it has turkey and apples, obviously, but mozzarella cheese and aioli as well."

"*Denki*, Patience. You choose."

After some banter as to who would choose, they decided to have half of each variety. Patience was in the act of lifting her sandwich to her mouth, when she saw Simon walking down the other side of the street. He carried a blonde child on his hip, while he held the hand of another little girl. They were dressed identically and from where Patience sat, she could see how people would mistake them for twins.

All Patience could do was stare at them. Simon looked the same and yet different. Even from the distance, she could see he looked older, more tired. The little girls looked delightful. The old anger that Patience had lived with for years began to bubble again. *They should have been my girls*, she thought. *That should have been my life.*

Her *mudder* caught her gaze and followed it. She reached over and patted Patience's hand as they sat in silence and watched the three of them walk down the street.

Part of her wanted to run into the street and confront him, but that of course was inappropriate in front of his *kinner*, and besides, whatever would she say? Another part of her wanted to melt onto the floor of the cafeteria and disappear. She sat in silence watching her old love and his *dochders* through the window.

Finally, Patience and her *mudder* left the cafeteria and walked to Mr. Beiler's room. Patience felt ill, and her stomach was in a knot. How awful to see Simon again after all these years. She silently chastised herself for not being over Simon. She had to stop being selfish and think of her *vadder*. He'd had a heart attack after all, and he needed care.

Mr. Beiler was sitting up in bed beaming when Patience and her *mudder* walked into the room. "They tell me that I can leave today."

Mrs. Beiler clasped her hands together in delight.

Patience noted that her *vadder* had some of his old color back in his cheeks. *There's no point being guilty*, she told herself. *Now I just have to do the books for Datt's buggy shop and help out as much as I can, and make amends for my long absence that way.*

CHAPTER 6

Patience tried to shrug off her annoyance about being sent into town to buy some flour. Surely her *mudder* could have seen the supplies getting low, but that's just how her *mudder* had always been, so she shouldn't hold it against her. But now she was having to pay for her *mudder's* lack of organization. Truth be told, Patience was not really annoyed with her *mudder*; she was annoyed with the fact of having to go into town.

Patience had done her best to avoid going into

town and being amongst people. She did not want to have to answer the same questions people were always asking when they realized who she was. Who have you married; why have you come back here; how many *kinner* do you have? It was always the same questions, and the answers she had to supply them with filled her with a sense of helplessness. *Nee*, she wasn't married, and of course if she wasn't married, she couldn't have *kinner*, and she had been forced to come back because of her parents' situation. She had not come back to this place filled with sad memories through her own choice.

Hopefully, if she kept her head down and did not look at anyone, no one would recognize her. For now she would enjoy the breeze against her face and concentrate on the road ahead, as her borrowed horse, Blessing, clip clopped along the dirt-packed road.

She closed her eyes and enjoyed the feel of the

sun as it warmed her face. The day was a pleasant one, not too cold.

It was no use: try as she might, everything about this place reminded her of Simon. Inevitably, there was always some memory of Simon that would spring to mind with every farm she passed. The first farm she passed was the Yoders'. She remembered the singings that were mostly held at the Yoders' due to the size of their two enormous barns. Simon and she had been inseparable at those times. The next farm she passed belonged to the Shetlers, and they had an enormous pond at the bottom of their land. Every child from the community had skated on it when it iced over in the wintertime.

Patience's shoulders drooped. She would leave this place with its memories as soon as her *Daed* got better. They were once happy memories, her sweet memories of Simon, but now they were bittersweet. Now, she was surrounded by things which made her sad.

As Blessing turned a corner, Patience was filled with dread. It was her old *skul* teacher, Mrs. Duffy. She would have to speak to kindly, old Mrs. Duffy even though all she wanted to do was get into town, do her shopping, and get back home as soon as possible.

Mrs. Duffy was collecting her mail and squinted at Patience as she pulled the buggy to a halt.

"Mrs. Duffy, it's Patience Beiler."

"*Ach*, Patience, my dear child. I haven't seen you for many years."

Mrs. Duffy walked quickly toward her buggy and Patience knew that Mrs. Duffy would be in for a long chat. This is exactly the type of thing Patience had been dreading, but Mrs. Duffy was such a nice lady that Patience didn't really mind speaking to her. It was the questions that she was dreading.

After answering a slew of questions about

what she was doing and whether she had a
beau, a *mann*, or *kinner*, Blessing whinnied
loudly and Patience swung toward him in
fright. Patience had not thought to tie
Blessing up; after all, where would he go?
When her *mudder* had borrowed him for her
upon her return, Daniel and Nettie Glick had
said he was very well trained, and the only
thing he ever did wrong was to open gates.
Patience had only intended to speak to Mrs.
Duffy for a moment.

Patience noticed a wild look in Blessing's eyes
and made a lunge for the reins, but it was too
late. Blessing shied away from her, making a
leap sideways and Patience landed in the dirt
on the side of the road.

The next thing Patience knew was that Mrs.
Duffy was helping her to her feet while her
driverless buggy was trotting happily down
the road.

"I've got to get him." Patience bunched up her

dress in both hands and ran after Blessing as fast as she could.

"Whoa, whoa," she breathlessly called after him, hoping that would work. Blessing turned off the road onto a dirt track, slowing down his pace. Patience managed to catch up with him. "Why did you do that?" she asked Blessing, as she stretched out her hand for the reins. There was nothing that had set him off; no car had driven past and honked the horn. There had been no loud noise whatsoever, and certainly she saw nothing such as washing that had blown off Mrs. Duffy's line off and flapped past Blessing's face.

Just as she almost had the reins in her hands, Blessing sped up and walked forward with his eyes fixed on something in the distance. "What is it that you see?"

Blessing finally stopped, and Patience sighed with relief. "Don't you ever do that again," she scolded him. "You could've been hurt." Just then, she heard the voices of young children. She tied Blessing to a tree and made sure that it was a very good knot. "Don't you dare untie that knot and wander off," she said, shaking her finger at him.

Patience followed the sound of the children and came to a small creek. She saw two little Amish *kinner* giggling and talking to each other as they sat at the creek's edge.

"*Hullo.*"

The little girls stared up the creek's bank where she stood.

"*Hiya*," the older girl said.

Patience looked up and down the creek's edge and could see no adult. "Are you girls here by yourself?"

"We *runned* away," the smallest of the girls said and was then poked in the ribs by the older one.

The girls continued to stare at Patience. "Well," she said, walking closer toward them, "Who did you run away from?"

Movement out of the corner of her eye caused her to look up. Patience saw a *mann* running at a fast pace toward them. Patience's blood ran cold when she saw that this was not just any *mann*; this *mann* was Simon. An older Simon, but *jah,* this man was definitely Simon.

Her first instinct was to turn and run, but that would be childish, and besides, he'd already seen her.

Simon had not recognized her, as his eyes were fixed on the two little girls. He ran to them and hugged them both as he fought back tears. "What do you two think that you were doing?"

"We *runned* away," the little girl repeated.

"Hush; there's no such word," the older girl

reprimanded the smaller one, as Simon scooped them both up into his arms.

When he straightened, he looked at Patience. "You!" The exclamation was one of utter shock.

Patience remained silent. What would she say to this *mann*? The *mann* who professed his love to her then married another. There was nothing to say. Her parents had raised her to be polite so she cleared her throat and said, "Your *dochders*?"

He pressed his lips together and nodded. "This one's Sarah and this one's Katie."

They were sweet little girls; Patience could not deny that. "They said that they were running away."

"Things have been a bit different lately."

Patience raised her eyebrows. "I'm guessing different, bad, not different good?" If Patience could have kicked herself she would have. She knew he was a single *vadder* struggling to cope with two young *kinner*. "I'm sorry, I just meant that..."

"It's just that we've all got to adjust. Things are different." Then he added, "Neither good nor bad, I guess."

Patience looked to the ground; she had to get away from him.

"What's your name?"

Patience looked up at the oldest girl who was still in Simon's arms. Patience smiled and said, "My name's Patience."

"Are you *Datt's* friend?"

"You can talk well for a small girl," Patience said, avoiding the question.

"How is it that you're here?" Simon asked.

Patience did not know if he meant here in Lancaster County, or here down by the creek. She decided to answer as if he meant the latter, as that would be easier to explain. "I was just speaking to old Mrs. Duffy and my horse got away from me." Patience turned around to point to Blessing, but he was gone. "Oh, no, he's gone again."

Patience hurried back up the bank, and Simon followed her after he put the two girls on the ground and held their hands.

"There he is," the oldest girl said, pointing in the distance.

Patience turned back toward Simon and his girls. "Well, thank you, Simon. I best go and fetch him."

She turned and walked away from Simon and his girls after saying goodbye. As she walked toward Blessing, who thankfully was now standing still, munching some grass by the side of the road, she could feel Simon still watching her. She hoped he could not hear the thumping of her heart.

CHAPTER 7

Everyone in the community now knew that
Patience was back, so she hoped that she
would not have to repeat her life history one
more time to anyone. It was at the next
gathering on the second Sunday that she knew
she would see Simon again. It annoyed her
that her life now revolved around being afraid
of seeing Simon, when it once revolved
around being happy to see him.

Patience and her *mudder* had left her *vadder*
alone in the *haus* that day. He insisted that no

one need stay with him. He was always a stickler for never missing one church meeting. Now, however, he did have regular visits to the home from the ministers and the bishop who discussed *Gott* and the Scriptures with him.

Her *mudder* sat on the wooden bench beside her and just before the bishop began, she leaned closer to her and said, "See that woman there?"

Patience followed where her *mudder* was looking. "*Jah*. I see her but I don't know her; is she new here?"

"*Jah*. Her name's Sadie, and she wants to marry Simon Warner."

Patience was unprepared for the wave of sadness that at once flowed over her. "How do you know?" she gasped. It was a silly question, for Patience's *mudder* always found out the latest goings on. She rarely got the information incorrect.

"I've heard a thing or two."

"Does he like her?" Patience asked, noticing the hardness of the woman, with her sharp nose, dark eyes, and the strands of shiny, black hair that poked out from the top of her prayer *kapp*. She was older than Patience would have thought that Simon would prefer, but then again, what would she know of Simon's preferences? It was clear that even Simon did not know what he preferred, since he had told her that she was the only woman for him, yet then he had married another.

Her *mudder* whispered, "*Menner* don't know what they want. I thought you would have learned that by now."

Patience felt that it was a harsh thing for her *mudder* to say, and it cut her deeply. Yet, her *mudder* could well be right. Maybe Simon was the same as all *menner*, and if what her *mudder* said was true, then no *mann* knew what he wanted.

65

Simon had said he loved her, and after she was gone for a short while, he had married someone she had once thought was her best friend. It had been a double betrayal and had left her feeling dark and alone. "Are they courting?"

Her *mudder* looked at her and then looked away after nodding her head sharply. "Sadie wants everyone to think so at least, but I don't know the truth of the matter."

Patience was annoyed with herself: annoyed with herself for finding him still attractive when she saw him down by the creek. Had she thought that she might have a second chance with him? In the back of her mind, she must have had a little hope that they could revive what they once had. Now, those hopes were dashed. Even though it had only been a tiny flicker of a hope, it left Patience feeling the same as she had when her best friend, Waneta, broke the news to her that she was betrothed to Simon all those years ago.

Patience compared Waneta and Sadie in looks. Sadie looked much older than Waneta, but then again, it had been a while since Patience had seen Waneta. They were both mere girls when Patience left the community. *I'd say Sadie is much older than Waneta would have been*, she thought.

As if she knew that she was thinking about Simon, her *mudder* leaned closer once again. "He needs a *mudder* for those two *kinner* of his."

Patience shifted nervously on the hard, wooden bench. "I forgot to tell you; I met his *dochders* down by the creek."

Her *mudder's* jaw fell open. "You did? So you've talked to Simon?"

Patience shrugged. "Well, I've kind of talked to him; I had to leave off in the middle and go and fetch Blessing. He got away again."

"Oh, that Blessing; he has a mind all of his own."

"Seems to have." It was because of Blessing that she ran into Simon when she did, but she would have run into Simon sooner or later.

Her *mudder* broke through her thoughts. "I look after the girls weekly on the day when Simon's *mudder* can't. I haven't since you've been home because I didn't want to upset you."

Patience was taking in what her *mudder* was saying, but she was also looking at Simon and Sadie as they spoke to each other before they went their separate ways to sit on separate sides of the room for the church meeting. As always, the *menner* were on one side, and the women on the other. Something within her wanted to know what kind of a woman Sadie was, but she stopped herself thinking such useless thoughts. Simon was none of her concern any more: in fact, he had not been any of her concern for some time. She wanted to have a man of principles, not a man who promised something one day and then totally forgot it the next. *Jah*, the man she married, if she ever did, would be a man who took his pledges seriously. A kind and strong man, a *mann* who follows *Gott*, just like her *daed*.

What the ministers said during their preaching, Patience could not say, as her mind was elsewhere.

As the women busied themselves getting the meal after the service, Patience did her best to stay away from Simon. She kept a close eye on his whereabouts to make sure she would be far away.

Patience saw that Sadie was bringing Simon's two *dochders* to the meal table. The older one broke free of Sadie's hand and ran toward Patience.

"You're the lady from the creek," she said shyly.

Patience smiled at the small girl and bent down to speak to her. "*Jah*, that's right. I hope you haven't tried to run away again."

Before Katie could speak, Sadie was beside the little girl and grabbed hold of her hand. "I told you if you do that again, I shall punish you. When I'm holding your hand, you must walk nicely, like a lady. Is that understood?"

Patience could see Katie swallow hard before she said, "*Jah*. Can I stay with this lady instead of you?"

Sadie looked Patience up and down. "Please forgive these children. They're quite unruly."

"*Nee*, they're fine. I'm Patience Beiler."

Sadie nodded her head. "I heard you'd come back. I'm Sadie Lengacher. I moved to the community with my *mudder* and *vadder* just over a year ago, when my *vadder* retired from farming."

Katie, the smaller girl, tugged on Sadie's over-apron. "Me stay with the lady."

"Can we both stay with the lady?" the older girl asked.

Sadie looked furious. "*Nee,* you must both stay with me, and if you misbehave again, I'll have your *daed* punish you."

"I don't mind looking after them if you want to go speak to people or something," Patience said, feeling sorry for the two little mites. They obviously didn't seem to care much for Sadie.

"*Nee, denki.* They're *my* responsibility." Sadie gave a thin-lipped smile which did not reach her eyes. She firmly took hold of the two girls' hands, and marched them away, almost faster than their little, chubby legs could go.

As they were being dragged away, Patience heard the little one say once more, "Me stay with the lady."

CHAPTER 8

Of all the things she enjoyed about coming home, her *vadder's* buggy shop was one of her favorites. It brought back plenty of pleasant memories. She could still remember standing on her tiptoes, passing the tools to her father as they chatted about everything under the sun.

He could tell her everything about a particular buggy, when it was made, if it had been in a wreck, even who made it. "A buggy should last thirty years," he always said.

Patience wished that she had tried harder to memorize all those stories. She would have been quite the buggy expert by this time. Of course, had she been a boy, then she would likely be running the place by now.

She shook her head and gave the old heater at the entrance two quick whacks. She smiled as it grumbled and kicked in to bathe the area in steady warmth. The thing had to be at least as old as she was, although it would've only been in the buggy shop from the time that the bishop had given her *vadder* permission to have electricity in there. It had rust spots everywhere, and its power cord was taped up in two places. It rattled and shook in its rickety frame, and reeked of charred dust every time it was turned on.

Her *vadder* had refused to toss the thing out, even when people had offered to buy him a new one. He often said the old rust bucket got him through many a cold afternoon when the weather was rough. Sometimes he treated it more like a *familye* pet than an old machine. No matter what anyone said, he refused to throw it out.

"They just don't make machines like it anymore," he said. "It's an example of good workmanship. Never throw out anything you can fix, Patience."

She patted the top of the machine and addressed it aloud. "Too bad people are harder to fix than machines."

Coming back to town had drudged up a lot of memories she thought she had put out of her mind. Seeing Simon's girls had driven home how much she had lost back then, although she thought of it almost every day: getting married, having *kinner*, raising a family. All her dreams had been shattered in one fell swoop. She had taken off to her *aenti's*, running from her problems. It had been a terrible choice, of course. In doing so, she had thrown out the good with the bad.

Patience sighed as she turned her back on the old heater. With a shake of her head, she thought that some things just couldn't be fixed. She had been gone so long, that she was practically a stranger in her own community. Simon had moved on to have a *familye* of his own; that was apparent. The thought that he had done so, not long after she moved away, caused her pain.

Still, what was done, was done. There was no time for regrets now.

A buggy rumbled at the entrance, and she snapped herself back into the present. She adjusted her prayer *kapp* and stepped out with her most welcoming smile, glad for the distraction from her thoughts.

Patience stopped dead in her tracks as she saw Simon standing there. His startled expression reminded her of a deer in caught in the headlights, wanting to run but too stunned to move. She knew the feeling rather well at the moment.

Patience recovered first and cleared her throat. She silently scolded herself for letting it get to her. How many times had she played out speaking to him again? How many speeches had she rehearsed? How many remarks in case he said anything? She shouldn't feel so jittery and out of sorts just by looking at him.

There were in the same, small community. They attended the same church meetings every other week. Their *mudders* were *gut* friends. Her *mudder* minded his *kinner* once a week. Of course, she was going to run into him time and time again, but just knowing that fact did not make it any easier.

Patience tried to muster her most professional, detached voice. "*Hullo*, Simon. What can I do for you?"

Simon jumped when she spoke. "I, err, the

buggy. I need to order new wheels. I was expecting Jake to be here?" He said it as a question rather than as a statement.

Patience shook her head. "This is Jake's day off."

She fought down a childish desire to throw a handful of snow at him. "I can order wheels for you."

"Perhaps I should come back when Jake's here." His voice was hesitant.

Patience looked at him. Simon looked good. She caught herself trying to smooth down her over-apron. "As you wish," she said.

"Is that all you are going to say?" Simon demanded.

Patience just looked at him.

"Patience!"

She jumped at the intensity and authority in his voice. In spite of herself, her heart clenched as she stared into his eyes, sad and searching. What did he see when he looked into her eyes, she had to wonder. The sadness in his eyes almost made her want to forget everything.

What did he want her to say? She had done nothing wrong; he was the one who had dated Waneta behind her back. "What else is there to say?" she said aloud.

Simon's lips moved silently, and he stammered, at a loss for words. He sighed in resignation, a bit of light dimming in his eyes. "I don't know," he finally said.

Patience forced a smile as she tried to ignore the pang of disappointment. She didn't know what she expected. She had no reason to think they could change what had happened. And she was not naive enough to expect a miracle to mend her broken heart. There were no explanations that could erase the past, and make everything better. Nothing.

Her eyes suddenly blurred. She quickly swept at her eyes, and then wiped the moisture onto her skirt. Simon was still looking at her, so Patience felt she should say something. "Your girls are *wunderbaar*."

"*Denki*."

There was another awkward silence, so after a while, Patience added, "I think highly of them."

"But not me, right?"

Patience took a step back at the bitterness of his tone. Hurt and annoyance rose within her. He had no right to get indignant over her opinion of him, none at all. It was entirely justified.

"I think you are a hard worker. And a *gut vadder*. You clearly try to do right by your girls. Considering everything, isn't that enough?"

"Enough?" His voice cracked. "We were engaged, Patience. You were going to be my *fraa*. You were coming back from vacation. You said you couldn't wait to see me. You couldn't wait to come home."

"I know!" she snapped. She took in a deep breath. This was no good; there was no point going over old ground. Why did he bring it up? Didn't he know that she knew about him and Waneta? Why wouldn't he just go away and leave her alone?

"Patience, what happened? I loved you. I never stopped loving you. Not even when you left me without a word. I didn't even know what to do with myself, I loved you so much. What changed between us?"

Patience took a deep breath. How dare he! "How could you, Simon? I really thought there was nothing and no one that could come between us."

Patience brushed her hand over her eyes. She squared her shoulders as she looked him in the eye. Her face burned red as the feeling of

shame and betrayal welled up to the surface.
"Just go, Simon, go!"

Simon hurried out of the buggy shop, more
confused than ever. He was angry with himself
for speaking frankly to Patience. How he had
managed to live with so many years of
frustration was beyond him. Why had
Patience run off all those years ago? He had
never found out. Clearly, she had been angry
with him, but for what? It was a mystery back
then, and it was still a mystery now.

Simon rubbed his chin. He used to think that
Patience merely had cold feet, but now he
could see that she was truly angry with him.
He had never believed Waneta when she told
him that Patience had fallen in love with
another *mann*. Clearly, Patience believed that
he had done something wrong. If only she

would tell him what he was supposed to have done, so it could all be straightened out.

Simon sighed and shook his head. If only Patience had told him, six years ago, what she thought he had done. That would have saved years of heartbreak, and he would be married to Patience now, and would have avoided a loveless marriage to Waneta. Still, he had his girls, and he thanked *Gott* for that.

CHAPTER 9

"A girlfriend?" Simon's *mudder*, Mary, gasped in shock, her eyes wide.

"*Jah*, that's what Patience finally told me yesterday." Patience's *mudder*, Annie, set down a plate of whoopie pies. "She was red eyed when she came home yesterday. It looked like she had been crying a good while. Goodness knows what brought everything up all of a sudden. But apparently she and Simon met at the buggy shop and had words about what happened six years ago."

Patience's *mudder*, Annie, was herself still trying to piece everything together. It had been a terrible shock when Patience spilled out everything that had happened to make her leave after her accident and go to her *Aenti's* in Ohio. Annie could only imagine what was going through Mary's mind, hearing that her own son, Simon, had been accused of having a girlfriend behind Patience's back.

"And Patience never said a word?" Mary asked, sounding vexed as she picked up a whoopie pie. "In all that time?"

Annie shook her head. "*Nee*, not so much as a peep, not in all these years. Anytime I ever tried to ask, she would change the subject, or have some excuse to get off the phone. Eventually, I stopped asking, and waited for her to be ready to talk about it on her own. But until last night, it never came."

"But my son, Simon, would never do that to Patience, Annie."

"*Jah*, I know that. You raised a good *mann*, Mary," Annie assured her. She gave a saddened smile as she shuffled the deck to prepare for their game, Dutch Blitz. It was a tradition had they started, to get past that time. Annie had hurt badly when her daughter Patience had gone to live with *Aenti* Carrie in Ohio, and only Simon handy to blame. She couldn't say she had always been fair to the man back then. It nearly cost her and Mary a forty year friendship, but by the grace of *Gott*, they had worked things out.

"We came back from vacation early."

Mary nodded. "I remember that."

Annie slowly dealt out their hands as she spoke. "*Jah*, we came back early. Patience at once went to your *haus* to see Simon."

Mary waved for her to continue. This part they both knew just fine. They'd debated what could have happened many times. Simon said he hadn't seen or heard from Patience before he saw her in the hospital.

Annie continued. "Well, she went to Farm Hill café, where you told her Simon was, and saw him with Waneta."

"Waneta?" Mary's tone was incredulous. Her mouth fell open when Annie gave a nod of confirmation. "But Waneta was just one of the *youngie* on *rumspringa*, along with Simon and Patience."

Annie simply shrugged.

"Well, what happened after that?"

"I'm getting to that." Annie put down the cards. "I'm still trying to make heads and tails of it myself."

She tapped the Wood Pile of cards to her right as she gathered her thoughts. "Apparently Patience went away by herself for a while, and when she came back, she saw

Waneta at a bakery. Waneta was alone - well, without Simon, but with some *Englischer* girls. Waneta told Patience that she and Simon had been seeing each other in secret, that it had all happened suddenly, and that they were planning to get married."

"Now that's a lie!" Mary protested. "What else did Waneta say to Patience? *Sell is nix as baeffzes!*" *That is nothing but trifling talk.*

"That's all Patience told me," Annie said. "But apparently, Waneta was convincing, so convincing, in fact, that Patience sped off and wrecked the truck. That's why she was in the hospital."

Mary gasped, and her hand flew to her throat. "Waneta caused Patience's accident? Why, she could've been killed. And to think that Patience ran away because of Waneta. And why would Patience believe such a fool story like that about Simon?" Confusion and anger shone in Mary's eyes as Dutch Blitz, the card game, was all but forgotten. "Why didn't she say anything? Why wouldn't she have said anything to Simon?" She started to rise, slapping down her cards. "Where is she? I'm going to talk to her right now and tell her the truth."

"You'll do no such thing." Annie's voice snapped with such authority that Mary froze in place. Annie continued, her tone more gentle. "Sit down. Patience couldn't have assumed anything less. She was young, don't forget, and apparently Waneta was entirely convincing. It's my fault; if I wasn't a bad *mudder* she would've told me all this at the time and we could've straightened it all out."

Mary sat down quietly. "*Nee*, you can't possibly think anything like that." Mary said gently, reaching out to pat her friend's hand and give it a squeeze. "Mothers always blame themselves. There was nothing you could've done."

Annie wiped her eyes with her free hand and sniffled, using the edge of her apron to dab at her face as she composed herself.

"I feel bad saying this as Waneta has now gone to be with *Gott*, and all," Mary said, "but I never much cared for her. I could never understand why Simon married her. There was never an ounce of love between them, and she was always yelling at Simon. She was a mean one, all right." Mary rubbed her temples. "She obviously wanted Simon for herself, so lied to Patience to drive a wedge between them."

They ate in silence a moment, leaving the cards on the table. The light slowly brightened as the sun dipped into late afternoon.

"So what now?" Mary asked as they started a new hand.

"Well, as I see it," Annie began as she poured them both some *kaffi*, "Patience and your son, Simon, had words about what happened back then. He's likely angry she ever thought something like that of him. That is, if he even knows what happened. And Patience has been heartbroken too long to realize that she was wrong."

Mary studied her good friend. She knew the look in her eyes all too well. "Annie, what are you plotting this time?"

Annie gave Mary a conspiratorial look. "Just a little head cold on the day I watch Simon's girls. Just a little nudge, that's all. What happens after that, happens. It's up to Simon and my *dochder* whether they try to fix this mess that Waneta left them with."

"Aren't you forgetting one thing?" Mary pointed out.

Annie frowned. "What's that?"

"Sadie."

"*Ach, jah*. Well, never you mind about Sadie. '*All the ways of a man are pure in his own eyes, but the Lord weighs the spirit. Commit your work to the Lord, and your plans will be established,'"* Annie quoted.

Mary rolled her eyes and wagged her finger at her friend. "Scripture smart, Annie!"

CHAPTER 10

Her *mudder* was right. It was a perfect day for ice skating. It brought back memories, especially of the winter days when things were so much less complicated. It would be so nice to go back to those days. Patience would have been happy to mind the girls even if her *mudder* had not suddenly come down with a head cold that morning.

"Miss Patience, look," Katie, the younger of the girls called. Patience looked up from tying her skates to watch the petite girl wobble and weave across the ice. Sarah was right beside her, skating slowly to watch over her sister.

"You're doing great!" Patience stood and carefully balanced herself on the edge of the ice. "You girls are naturals!"

Sarah smiled as she held her *schweschder's* hand, keeping her upright. Katie beamed and shuffled her skates. "I want to go faster!" she cried.

Patience smiled, sliding over beside them. "You sound like your *vadder*. He was always racing on this pond. Did he teach you girls how to skate?"

"*Grossmammi* taught us," Sarah answered. Katie nodded her head energetically as she tried to skate ahead, wriggling her head to try to escape her sister. Sarah gave a little shrug. "*Datt's* been busy."

"And our *mudder* went to heaven," Katie called out.

"I heard." Patience's tone was filled with sympathy. It must have been so hard on the girls to have lost their *mudder*. The younger one had never known her, and the older one would probably not be able to remember. It was time for a swift change of the subject. Now wasn't the time to remind them of such sad things. "You know, I'm surprised your *vadder* didn't teach you. He was very good at skating when we were young."

That had their attention. Both girls stopped in their tracks, forcing Patience to brake.

"Daddy could skate?" Katie asked, her blue eyes wide with awe.

"Really? What could he do?" Sarah asked

This was the most excited Patience had ever seen the girls. They truly did admire their father, she realized. She hadn't doubted it before, but just how much they adored him was made clear by the expressions on their little faces.

She smiled as she thought back. Simon had looked so handsome those days. She remembered how snow powder stuck to his hair and his hat, and the looks of determination on his face. She remembered the way he flew across the little pond as if he were skating on the wind itself. Sometimes it was too easy to forget the simple things.

"Your *vadder* and I often competed with each other back then," Patience said with a chuckle. "We would find all sorts of silly things to do, and see who could do them better. We did so many stunts on this ice, that's a wonder we didn't get grounded the whole winter."

The girls giggled as they listened, especially the idea of *Datt* and Miss Patience getting grounded.

"One year, my friends and I decided to see who could pull off the best tricks. I raced across the ice and jumped into a double spin. I managed to land safely." Patience stopped speaking and smiled softly at the memory. "Then it was your *vadder's* turn. He raced and raced around the ice until he couldn't go any faster. Then he jumped."

She smiled and paused as the girls looked over the ice in wonder.

"Daddy flew?" Katie asked excitedly, bouncing on her feet.

Patience quickly caught her as she lost her balance. "*Jah*. Higher than we ever saw anyone do."

Sarah's face brightened.

Patience smiled. She didn't tell them that Simon also missed the pond in the landing. She had been in awe of that moment, but she had teased him back then, after making sure he hadn't gotten hurt face-planting in that snowdrift. It was a wonder they lived to see adulthood with some of the stunts they pulled.

"Did he spin?"

"*Nee*." Patience found it easy to think of Simon with his *dochders* there. For some reason, reminiscing about him didn't bring the pain it usually brought.

"Did he crash through the ice?"

"*Nee, nee*, nothing like that."

It seemed like the questions were never going to end. They went round and round the little pond until Patience lost count. They wanted to know stories about their *vadder*. They had dozens of questions about when their father was a child. Patience did her best to answer, although she wasn't able to answer everything.

It took her a while to realize that they were skating much more proficiently, each holding one of her hands as they chattered away. They had such bright smiles as they skated along, cheeks red from the cold, and little flakes stuck on their bonnets.

"How about we go back to my *haus* for cocoa?"

Both girls cheered agreement, clumsily pulling Patience toward the edge of the pond. She helped them change into their snow boots. It took a few minutes, as it had been a long time since she helped anyone get out of ice skates. "Your *vadder* is going to pick you up soon."

"*Nee, nee,*" Katie whined, as she looked up at Patience pleadingly.

"Can *Datt* just come and skate with us?" Sarah begged.

"I'm pretty sure he already has plans for you." Patience smoothed out a tangled hair on the smallest one. "But I really had a great time. You girls are just wonderful."

"Will you take us skating again one day soon?" Sarah asked, looking at Patience wistfully.

Patience melted at her sweet expression. Who could say no to that face? "I don't see why not." She looked up at the wisps of clouds in the sky. She had always wanted to be a mother, and after spending a couple hours with the girls, she wondered what kind of mother she would be. She wondered what her children would be like one day. She wondered when she would teach them to skate. She wondered if they would be just as interested as Simon's *kinner* when she told them about her childhood.

Patience imagined Simon cooing over a newborn *boppli*, totally absorbed by tiny fingers and toes. At once, Patience shook her head to drive away such thoughts. She knew better than to entertain thoughts like that.

"*Jah*, of course I will," she promised them, stomping her feet to keep the cold off them.

"Are you going to marry *Datt*?" Katie asked.

Patience tried not to choke at the question.

Sarah interrupted. "*Jah*, please marry *Datt*, Miss Patience. Then Miss Sadie will go away."

"I don't like Miss Sadie. She's mean." Katie kicked at the snow with her little boot as she stared at the ground.

"*Shhh*! *Datt* says not to call people names," Sarah scolded, but her words sounded strangely hollow in Patience's ears.

Patience sat back down so that she was almost eye level to them. "I'm sure she's not all that bad."

"She is so mean!" Katie insisted, ignoring her *schweschder's* attempts to hush her. "She talks in a mean voice when Daddy isn't there."

"She called us brats," Sarah added as she looked away. "She called me a monster because I spilled cereal on the floor."

Patience felt her face flush as the girls talked. Her *mudder* had never had trouble with the girls when she minded them; in fact, she was always saying how good they were. She couldn't see them doing anything that would make them deserve such treatment. That was uncalled for.

Patience knew she should change the subject, but her heart ached at the sight of tiny Katie, her little lip quivering. "Did you tell your *daed*?"

Katie pouted and then shook her head.

"Miss Sadie said I threw it down on purpose," Sarah said. "*Datt* says we have to try to get along with Miss Sadie."

Patience took a calming breath. Her first instinct was that she could not just sit back and ignore something like that, especially with how upset this was apparently making the girls. Yet, at the same time, she knew only too well that it wasn't any of her business. She was quite sure that Simon would not appreciate her interference into his personal life.

"Can't *you* marry Datt?" Katie asked again, with wide, pleading eyes.

Patience sighed. "*Nee*, but I can take you skating again soon, and I'll be here every time you come and stay with my *mudder*. What do you think of that?"

That seemed to cheer up the girls considerably. They were back to their usual, chattering selves by the time Patience got them back to the *haus*.

CHAPTER 11

There was a knock on the door and Patience
jumped in surprise. It was late; the sun had
gone down, and Patience was sure that her
familye was not expecting company. Her *daed*
needed his rest, and the community knew
that. She was wearing her warm nightgown
and was lying on the couch, eating popcorn,
and reading the *Christenpflicht* prayer book.

As Patience stood, she reached up to her head
and ran her fingers through her long hair.
There was no time to put on her prayer *kapp*.

Besides, who could be knocking this close to bedtime?

Patience paused by the front door and prepared to open it, after throwing her coat around her. She took a deep breath, and then pulled the door open.

There stood Simon's *dochders*, Sarah and Katie. The two little girls were holding hands, and both of them were dressed in their nightgowns. Tears were rolling down Katie's cheeks.

Sarah stepped forward, letting go of her *schweschder's* hand and wrapping her arms around Patience's leg. "We want to live with you," she said, as she too began to cry.

Patience bent down and hugged the girl, and then reached for Katie and pulled her into a hug as well.

"What's going on with you two? Where is your *vadder*?"

"Home," Sarah sniffed. Katie appeared to be crying too hard to speak.

"Hurry girls; you're frozen. Come inside by the fire." Patience soon had the girls sitting by the fire, and she wrapped warm blankets around them. She took off their soaked boots and placed them by the fire.

"Does your *vadder* know you're here?" she asked, and at once thought it was a silly question - of course Simon wouldn't let his *dochders* leave the *haus* alone and especially not at night. "I'm going to go to the barn and call your *vadder* and tell him that you're here, so he doesn't worry about you. Then I'll come back and make you both a nice cocoa, okay?"

The girls nodded. As Patience started for the barn, she was suddenly anxious that the girls might run away again, so gave them her bowl of popcorn.

"Popcorn!" Katie said excitedly as she sniffed loudly, working to fight off the tears.

"Now, the two of you stay here and eat while I call."

The girls stuck their stubby fingers into the bowl and pulled handfuls of popcorn to their mouths, dropping most of the kernels onto the front of their nightgowns and the couch.

Patience hurried to the barn, and called Simon. She figured he would be waiting by the phone in his barn for news of the girls. She was correct; he answered at once. He sounded harried, his voice louder than usual, his tone sharp.

"*Hullo?*" he said.

"The girls are here," Patience said, figuring that was a good thing to lead with.

"Oh, thank goodness," Simon said. "What? How? Are they okay?"

"*Jah, jah*, don't worry; they're fine, but they're very upset," Patience said. "Why don't you let them stay here tonight, and I'll find out why they're upset. I don't think they need to be in trouble right now."

"Patience, they left the *haus* at night and in the cold," Simon said with a catch in his voice. "They *are* in trouble."

"I know," Patience said. "Just let them be in trouble tomorrow. Please," she added.

There was a pause, a sigh, and then Simon spoke. "Okay."

"*Denki*. You can call for them in the morning, okay?"

"*Alright. Denki*, Patience. You're a *gut* friend."

Patience did not know how to respond. She simply said, "*Denki*," and then hung up. She looked at the phone for a moment. Her heart was racing, and butterflies were playing havoc with her stomach. She shook her head and darted back out into the cold.

When she returned to the living room, she

found the girls still on the couch, eating popcorn.

"Did you call *Datt*?" Sarah asked as Katie looked at her with wide eyes.

Patience nodded. "*Jah*."

"Is he mad at us?"

"A little," Patience said truthfully. "He was worried about you. He said you left without him knowing."

Sarah nodded as Katie spoke up. "We wanted to leave. We don't want her for a new *mudder*."

"Who?" Patience asked the girl.

"Miss Sadie," Sarah said. "She told us she was going to be our new *mudder*."

Patience frowned. "What do you mean?"

Sarah looked to Katie for a moment and then turned back to Patience. "Miss Sadie said she was going to be our new *mudder*."

Patience was trying to take it all in. "Miss Sadie told you she was going to be your new *mudder*?"

"*Jah*," Sarah said. "She said *Datt* loved her, and she loved him. She told us she would get married to him, and be our *mudder*."

With this, the girls both started crying again in earnest. Patience sat down on the couch next to the girls and took them both onto her lap. She hugged them close and kissed each of their foreheads.

"I should make you that cocoa now," Patience said in an attempt to distract the girls. She had no idea what else to say about the situation with Simon and Sadie.

"We don't want her to be our *mudder*," Sarah sniffled. "We love our *vadder*; we don't have to have a new *mudder*," Sarah said.

Katie spoke up. "And if we did, we'd rather it be you, Patience."

Patience looked at the girls, and felt at a complete loss. Whatever could she say? "I'll make you both cocoa and you finish that popcorn."

"*Jah, denki*." Katie tipped her head up and smiled at Patience.

When Patience returned with the cocoa, she sat between both girls. "You girls don't need to be upset about anything."

Katie sniffed. "But Miss Sadie said that she was going to marry *Datt,* and that would make her our new *mudder,* and we don't like her."

Sarah dug Katie in the ribs.

"Well, it's true," Katie said, as she turned to face her older *schweschder.*

Patience was miserable at the thought of Simon marrying again. She had once been sure that he was the only *mann* for her, and she had been just as sure that he felt the same way about her. How silly she had been. He and

Waneta had been together and she hadn't even known. He had married Waneta. Her *mudder* had told her that Waneta had been totally unsuited to him. Would Simon make the same mistake twice? Surely not, not when his own *dochders* displayed so much dislike for the woman. And it was clear that Sadie did not think too much of them in turn. Patience searched her mind for words of comfort for the two small girls, but no words came to mind. She could not find the words to tell them what their *vadder* would or would not do.

All her feelings for Simon came flooding back. She knew that *Gott* had one *mann* for every woman, and she knew that Simon was the *mann* for her. So why did things turn out as they had? She knew she could never love anyone else. It was bad enough that Simon had betrayed her when they were young and on *rumspringa*, but she had lately been putting that down to the silliness of youth.

Patience realized at this very moment that she had been hoping fervently that she and Simon would rekindle their old romance. She thought she had seen signs that he still felt the spark for her. So why was he going to marry Sadie? It made no sense.

Patience reached across and touched their hands. "*Ach,* you're both warmer now. You should not have come out on a cold night like this. You can sleep here tonight, and your *vadder* said he'd come and get you tomorrow."

"Can you tell him not to marry Miss Sadie?"

Patience looked at the two girls' faces staring up at her. She wanted to promise them that their *vadder* would not marry someone unsuitable. She wanted to promise them that when and if he married again that it would be someone whom they adored. Yet, of course, she could not make any such promises or even give them any assurances. "Your *vadder* has to make his own choices. Perhaps you can tell him how you feel tomorrow when he comes to collect you."

The two girls looked at each other, and Patience was worried that they might cry again.

"Come on, drink your cocoa. It's past your bedtimes."

"Can't you marry *Datt*?" Katie piped up again.

Patience sighed. She would like nothing more than to marry Simon. "It doesn't work like that," she said.

Katie turned her little face up at her. "How does it work?"

Patience had often wondered the same thing. It would be nice if love came with a rule book like a recipe. A cup of kindness, a spoonful of understanding, and a pinch of trust and ending in a lovely relationship, but life and love were far too complicated to define. "It's complicated," was all she could say. "Now, come on; it's late. I'm going to give the kitchen a quick clean while you finish your cocoa."

Later, when their fingertips were sliding along the bottom of a buttery, empty bowl, and their eyelids were fluttering shut, Patience stood, and carried each girl in turn upstairs to her bedroom.

Her parents had guest rooms, but the beds were not made up, so Patience took the girls to her room and laid them side by side on the bed. She then went to the bathroom and brushed her teeth. When she returned, both of the little girls were sleeping. *Poor little mites,* she thought. *Such a long way for them to walk in the cold.*

Patience turned off the light and climbed into bed as well. She lay on her side of the bed facing the girls.

The moon was full that night, and its silver light fell through the window and across half of the bed. Patience couldn't take her eyes off the girls. She felt a strong urge to take care of them, to keep them safe, to make them happy. She watched them as she herself grew tired, and then when she couldn't force her eyes to stay open any longer, she shut her eyes and drifted off to sleep.

CHAPTER 12

Simon hung up the phone and turned to
Sadie, who was hovering in the door of his
barn. "Was that them?" she asked.

"*Jah*, it was Patience," Simon said. "They went
to her *haus*."

An unmistakable flash of annoyance ran
across Sadie's features, but she covered it just
as quickly. "Why did they go there?" she
asked, unsuccessfully trying to hide the
jealousy in her tone.

"I don't know," Simon said. "They like her. Now I must call the police back and tell them they've been found." He reached for the phone, but the sound of a car outside prevented him. Simon pulled the heavy door open and hurried over to the uniformed police officers who had just gotten out of the car.

"I'm sorry," Simon said. "I just found out where my daughters are. They're safe."

The female police officer tucked her hat under her arm. "You found them?"

Simon nodded. "They went to a friend's house nearby," he said. "I don't know why yet; I'm not sure if they were upset or what, but I'm sorry you drove out all this way."

The police officer smiled. "I'm just glad you found them," she said. "Kids are crazy; who knows why they do anything."

The other police officer was a gruff looking, older man with a sizable paunch, and a thick, gray mustache. "When my boy was young, he flushed everything he could get a hold of down the toilet. Watches, earrings, mostly shiny things I guess. Did it until he was four. Who knows why."

Simon nodded, relieved that the officers were not annoyed. They all shook hands, and then the officers drove away. He saw that Sadie had headed for his *haus*.

"Aren't you going to go get them?" Sadie asked from the porch.

"*Nee*, they're going to stay with Patience for tonight," Simon told her as he approached her. As he did so, the woman reached for his arm and stopped him.

Sadie clutched at his arm. "You aren't serious, are you? They ran away; they need to be punished."

Simon was annoyed. "Something upset them, so there's no use going over there while they're still upset. They'll talk to Patience more than they would talk to me."

"They'll talk to you. Or me," Sadie snapped.

Simon folded his arms across his chest and the movement dislodged Sadie's hand. "I'm thankful for your help during this, but it's getting late. You had better be getting home."

Sadie shook her head. "*Nee*, I don't mind."

"Sadie, really," Simon said. "Go. It's fine."

Sadie stepped forward, put her hands on Simon's shoulders. "I won't leave a friend," she said.

Simon sighed, reached up and took her arms in his hands. "I think we should talk," he said.

He led Sadie to the couch and sat down. She sat next to him, a look of worry on her face.

"What is it?" she asked.

"I think you have the wrong impression here," Simon said, as kindly as he could.

"What do you mean?"

"I mean that I don't have feelings for you," Simon said, deciding that while he needed to be kind, he also needed to be blunt. Sadie was the kind of woman who would read into any little thing he conceded to her, so he could concede nothing. He had to make sure she knew he simply wasn't interested in her.

"I see," Sadie said. "You often take women out on dates that you aren't interested?"

Simon almost sighed, but he caught himself. "We haven't dated, Sadie. I just don't feel that way for you." The truth of the matter was that Sadie had pursued him relentlessly. He should have set things straight much earlier, but she had initially told him that she only saw him as a friend and wanted to help with the girls. He had stupidly thought she was just being community-minded.

Sadie stood up in an obvious temper. "I don't know what kind of game you were playing, but I guess it's better that it's over now, before I devote any more of my time to you or your brats of girls," she said.

"I wasn't playing a game," Simon said, rising as well. "I really wasn't. I want to be friends." He was upset that she had called his *dochders* "brats," but figured it was solely because she was so upset.

Sadie laughed, a high pitched laugh. "I have enough friends," she said, and then she spun on her heels and slammed the front door as hard as she could. Simon shook his head and then headed upstairs to his bedroom.

Later, Simon woke in the middle of the night. He sat up, his mouth dry and his throat scratchy. He climbed from his bed once more and went into the bathroom. He washed his face and then went back to his room. He lay down again, on his back, staring at the ceiling in the inky darkness. He thought of his girls, and then his mind went to Patience.

He thought back to when they dated, the fun the used to have. She was the one he was going to marry, the one woman for him, but then she had ended it all.

He thought about how safe it felt to have his *dochders* with Patience, and then he fell back to sleep.

CHAPTER 13

Patience awoke to someone shaking her shoulder. "Wake up; it's morning."

Patience opened one eye and saw the two girls standing over her. "It's morning?" She generally woke up early, but the sun wasn't even up. Patience looked across to the window past the girls and saw that the sun was only now ready to break over the horizon.

"We're hungry," Katie said.

Patience blinked a couple of times, and then

sat up. "I'd better get you something to eat then, but you must be quiet walking past my *mudder* and *vadder's* room. *My vadder* has been ill and needs his sleep."

The two girls had requested pancakes with syrup, and pancakes were also a favorite of Patience's. After the girls had eaten all the pancakes they possibly could, they helped Patience wash the dishes and wipe down the table.

"I'm not sure what time your *vadder* is coming to get you this morning, but would you both like to help me work in the garden?"

"*Jah*," both girls answered with excitement.

Patience was pleased that her *mudder* had some spare clothes for the girls due to the fact that she minded them once a week. They changed into the clothes and they all headed outside.

Patience loved spending time with the girls.

They had been so upset when they arrived, but they had quickly calmed down after popcorn and cocoa.

The morning sun was warm against their skin and Patience felt a glow in her heart when she looked at the two young girls. She wondered if she could love them anymore if they were her own *kinner*.

Patience spent most of the day in the garden with Simon's girls. It was not the season to plant seeds, but there were always plenty of weeds to pull out in the vegetable patch and in amongst the flowers in front of the *haus*. For some reason, the girls loved to pull out the weeds, and once Patience showed them how to dig around and loosen the soil and be sure to get all the roots, they giggled and held up each weed they pulled out that had roots. They had pulled out many weeds by the tops only, leaving the roots still in the ground.

At the sound of hoof beats, Patience's heart

beat in her chest just as loudly as the horse's hooves, at least to her mind. She looked up to see Simon's buggy heading toward her *haus*.

"It's *Datt*; it's *Datt*." Katie jumped up and down with excitement.

"*Shhh*," Sarah said to her younger schweschder. "We might be in trouble for running away."

Katie pulled a face.

Simon stopped the buggy and tied the horse up to the post outside the *haus* while Patience walked toward him, a girl either side of her, holding her hands.

Simon crouched down and opened his arms wide. The girls broke free and ran toward him. It was clear that they knew by the look on his face that they were not going to get into trouble.

Simon smiled over the top of their heads at her. "*Denki*, Patience."

"It's always a pleasure to watch the girls." She turned to Sarah and Katie. "Why don't you two go and fetch the gardening tools and place them back in the tool room?" she suggested.

"Okay," Sarah said. She took her younger *schweschder* by the arm and walked her back toward the garden.

"They're upset." Patience's words came out a little more aggressively than she wanted them to. "They ran away over something that Sadie told them."

Simon put his head to the side, and his eyebrows knitted in the center. "What did she say to them?"

"She said that she was going to marry you and become their *mudder*."

Simon stepped back from her and cast his eyes to the ground.

That's right; he can't look at me; it's the same as last

time, Patience thought. She folded her arms over her chest and waited for him to continue. Simon's faced flushed beet red but still, he did not speak. *I will stand here until nightfall if necessary*, Patience thought, *until he does speak.*

Simon finally met her eyes. "I need to tell you that I was never courting Sadie in the first instance. She was only ever a friend, in my mind at least, but it appears that she had other ideas from the very beginning. I set things straight with her last night."

Enormous waves of relief washed over Patience.

CHAPTER 14

Simon walked along Main Street, heading for Henry's Amish Buggy Shop. It just so happened that Patience's father was Henry, and she had begun doing the books for him since she moved back to town. She was an accounting whiz, and her father was not, so she had plenty of work to do to get him back on track. Simon found himself thinking of Patience as he walked, and he felt excited about the prospect of seeing her.

The shop was a squat place with a large lot for buggies waiting to be worked on. Simon made his way to the building and stepped inside. Jake was there working on a buggy. When Jake saw Simon standing near the large, open doorway, he turned and picked up a red rag to wipe his dirty hands.

"*Hiya*, Simon, your new wheels are on your buggy. I tucked the bill inside; get it to me when you can."

Simon laughed and shook the older *mann's* hand. "Will the new accountant be okay with that method of business, Jake? Letting customers pay whenever they can?"

"As long as they pay, I'll tell her to be okay with it," Jake replied with a laugh. "She's over in the office if you want to say *hullo* to her," he added with a knowing look in his eye.

Simon smiled and nodded, turning and heading for the office.

The door was shut to the crack, and Simon knocked on it softly before pushing it open. Patience was sitting behind an ancient desk loaded with papers. She had a laptop open in front of her, and she looked harried. She smiled when she saw Simon, setting a pen down and moving her hands to her prayer *kapp* to tuck a stray wisp of hair back under it.

"You look perfect," Simon said before he could stop himself, or consider the implications of saying such a thing.

Patience looked taken aback, and then smiled. "If Jake did something wrong, you have to talk with him. I'm strictly behind the scenes." Her tone was amused. "How are the girls?"

"*Gut, denki.* They're always asking to see you."

Before Patience could reply, the store phone rang. Simon watched her as she had a quick conversation, one that was obviously distressing to her.

She hung up, and Simon looked at her with concern. "Patience, what's wrong?"

"It's *Daed*," she said. "*Mamm* thinks he's had another heart attack. He's in the hospital. I'll have to call a taxi."

"I'll go and tell Jake what's happened, while you call a taxi," Simon said. "I'll go with you to the hospital."

"Will you?" she asked.

"Of course."

Later, as they stood in a corner of the waiting room, Simon saw that Patience's eyes were swimming with salty tears. She looked to Simon and broke down, the tears spilling over her eyelids and running down her cheeks, leaving wet trails along them. Simon stepped forward and wrapped his arms around her.

"I'm scared," she said, breathing against his neck.

"I know," Simon said, and that was all they said as they waited for the doctor to come and tell them more about her *vadder's* condition.

CHAPTER 15

Patience wondered how much longer Simon and she would have to wait in the stark room, waiting to hear about her *vadder's* condition. It seemed as if they had been waiting there for hours already. Patience felt Simon's eyes on her; she looked at him, and he smiled. She forced a smile back. Simon was trying his best to be comforting and she was grateful that he was there with her.

"I'll get us some *kaffi*." Simon stood up.

"*Nee*, please wait." Patience needed him by her side just in case someone delivered bad news.

"Of course, I'll wait. I just thought you could do with some distraction."

Patience gave a slight nod of acknowledgment that she had heard what he said, but just Simon being there was as much as a distraction that she could have. Her feelings for Simon for once in her life were secondary in her mind. Her *vadder* had been sick for a time, but what if he did not make it? How would she handle it if they came and told her bad news?

Patience bit down hard on her lip. She could not cry; she had to be strong for her *mudder*.

"Why don't we say a prayer?"

Patience looked at Simon. "*Jah*, that would be *gut. Denki*."

She looked at Simon's eyes and a great deal of her fear melted away. How much this *mann* always made her feel so safe and protected when he was close to her. She closed her eyes, let out a deep breath, and waited for him to pray.

"May I hold your hand?"

Patience opened her eyes and her mouth at the same time. As soon as she realized her mouth was open, she quickly closed it. If he was going to pray, she could let him hold her hand. Her heart raced as she gave a quick nod and moved her hand slightly toward him.

Simon did not smile, and his expression did not change; it was as if he did this kind of thing every day. He covered her small hand with his large hand and then clasped his other hand over the top. "Dear *Gott*, we humbly come before You as Your servants. We ask that You show mercy upon Patience's *vadder* and above all that Your will be done in this hospital today. Only You know our comings and goings and only You know what is right for each and every one of us, so we ask that if it be Your will, that You restore Patience's *vadder* to health. Amen."

"Amen," Patience repeated and opened her eyes. She saw that Simon's eyes were still closed, and he still had her small hand clasped in between his two large hands. She did not want to snatch her hand away; she would have to wait until he released it.

Seconds later Simon opened his eyes and squeezed Patience's hand. "We must trust in *Gott*."

Patience nodded and marveled at his faith. This was the kind of *mann* that she wanted to be the *vadder* to her *kinner*. Tears brimmed in her eyes, and not for her *vadder* this time; the tears were for losing Simon to Waneta all those years ago, and tears at the uncertainty of her future.

Simon released Patience's hand just as her *mudder* walked into the waiting room.

Patience could tell by the look on her *mudder's* face that her *vadder* was going to be all right.

Patience led her *mudder* to a chair and sat down next to her.

"He's going to be okay, the *doktor* said. It was just his new medication."

Immediately Patience felt her whole body relax. "What was wrong with him?"

"He had some sort of an episode; the *doktor* called it a turn. They just need to adjust his medication, and he'll be fine. They're going to keep him here while they get the level of medication right."

Patience looked over at Simon, and he smiled warmly. Then she turned her attention back to her *mudder.* "Can I see him? Is he awake?"

"*Jah*, a few more moments and you can see him. The *doktor* is still in with him at the moment."

"What a relief," Patience said with her hands over her face. She knew that everyone has to die at some point, but her parents had a good many more years in them yet, she was sure of it.

"The *doktor* says that he needs to get some sort of exercise, and watch what he eats, no more cream or whoopee pies, that kind of thing."

"*Ach, Datt's* favorite foods," Patience said with a chuckle.

"Does he need to do anything else?" Simon asked.

"He needs to do some walking every day. The *doktor* suggested that he work up to two walks of around twenty minutes, twice a day."

Simon nodded. "We can see that he does that."

Did he just say 'we'? Patience wondered why he would say '*we*' as if they were a couple.

Patience could see that her *mudder* noticed Simon's comment as well. Nothing slipped by her *mudder*.

To hide her confusion, Patience said, "I'll peep in the room and see if the *doktor's* still in there." Patience walked down the corridor to her *vadder's* room, and peeped looked through the slim window just above the door handle. The doctor was nowhere to be seen.

"*Datt*." Patience walked quietly toward her *vadder*.

A faint smile touched his face, even though his eyes were barely open. "Patience." His words were a whisper.

"I won't stay long; I just wanted to see you." She bent over and gave her *vadder* a kiss on his forehead.

His eyes closed, and it was clear that he was too weak to speak. At that moment, a nurse came in the room. "The doctor's just given him something, so he'll be asleep for a while."

Patience nodded. "I'll come back later." She walked back to her *mudder* and Simon.

"He looks okay, *Mamm*."

"I'll stay with him a while longer."

"Don't hurry, *Mamm*. I'll keep your dinner warm for you."

Her *mudder* patted her on the shoulder and walked back to her *vadder's* room.

"*Denki* for staying with me, Simon. I don't know what I would've done without you here." Normally Patience would not have said such a thing to Simon, but it was true, and she could not deny it.

Simon smiled so warmly that the butterflies in Patience's stomach churned wildly. "Let's get some food into you. When was the last time you ate?"

Patience shrugged.

"There's a café here, best we have something here."

Once they were seated at the café, with sandwiches in front of them, Simon said, "You know, my girls like you very much."

Patience smiled at the mention of his two *dochders*. "I like them very much, too. They are very sweet and so well behaved."

"They used to be well behaved. I don't know what got into them the other night when they went to your *haus*."

"I think they feel some kind of comfort at my *haus* because *Mamm* has looked after them often."

Simon shook his head. "It's you they seem to find comfort in."

Patience flushed at his words, yet, as much as Patience loved his two *dochders*, they often reminded her of how Simon disregarded their intentions and had married Waneta suddenly. *Nothing makes sense; I was sure that he loved me all those years ago, and I think he might even love me now. But, what if I am wrong – again? Maybe he had acted on a youthful impulse when he asked Waneta to marry him. Everyone makes mistakes and more so in their youth. Jah, that must be it,* Patience thought hopefully.

CHAPTER 16

Patience and most of the other women in the community were in her parents' *haus*, baking for Emily Hershberger, who had recently given birth to twins. Emily's *mudder* and *grossmammi* were both ill, so it was up to the community to rally around and provide for Emily's *familye*.

Patience was busying herself with pot pie. She had just rolled out the dough and hung it in strips on the backs of the wooden kitchen chairs to dry before cutting it into square noodles.

"How is the pot pie coming along?" her *mudder* asked.

"Fine, *denki, Mamm*."

Her *mudder* nodded. "*Gut*. Will you be putting in potatoes or other vegetables along with the chicken and gravy?"

"Potatoes. There are plenty of them." She nodded over at one of the ladies who was mashing a mound of potatoes, and a pile of unpeeled potatoes sat nearby.

Her *mudder* nodded again. "Patience, I'm going to sit with your *vadder* now and read to him. Will you be able to provide *kaffi* and food for the ladies?"

"Sure, *Mamm*. No need to rush back; stay with *Datt* as long as you like." With that, her *mudder* left the kitchen and Patience looked around the room. One lady was making shoo fly pies; one lady was making *schnitz und knepp*, and two ladies were making whoopie pies in every color imaginable. Yet another lady was making chow-chow, a pickled vegetable relish. Patience had lost track of what the other ladies were making, but her *mudder's* kitchen was a hive of activity.

The women were working efficiently, and chatting with each other and laughing. Everyone, that is, except Sadie, who was keeping to herself and wearing a sour expression on her face.

After a while, Patience decided to make a pot of *kaffi* for the ladies. She jumped as Sadie came up behind her.

"So, Patience, how do you like being back home?"

Patience looked around into Sadie's cold eyes. "It's *gut*."

Sadie took a step closer and lowered her voice.

153

"Did you come back just because of your *vadder*?"

Patience frowned. She wondered where this line of questioning was going. "*Jah*, I came back because my *vadder* had taken ill; he had the heart attack."

"And nothing else?"

"Isn't that enough?" Patience hadn't meant her words to sound so abrupt, but she'd had enough of trouble-making females for one lifetime already. And while Sadie had not caused trouble yet, Patience felt quite sure that she was about to.

At any rate, Sadie did not appear to have taken offense at her comment for she pressed on. "So you didn't come back for Simon?"

Patience scrunched up her face. "Simon? *Nee*, of course not." She could not help but sigh. Patience turned back to making the *kaffi* but

Sadie tapped her on the shoulder. She turned around again.

"So you didn't come back because you heard that Simon and I were dating?"

Patience folded her arms across her chest. "No, I didn't hear that you and Simon were dating, not at all," she said. She hoped her cold tone would give Sadie the hint not to pursue her line of questioning, but it did not work.

"And so when did you last see Simon?" Sadie asked, narrowing her eyes.

"Look, Sadie," Patience said, "I don't wish to be rude, but that is none of your concern."

Sadie's face flushed beet red. "So he's told you about us?" she snapped. "Leading me on like that, and then saying we were never dating. Why, I helped him look after those little brats for quite some time, and that's all the thanks I got. And as for Simon, well, *er is weenich ad.*"

Patience was affronted. "Simon is not *a little off in the head* at all," she said. "And you must not call those darling, little girls 'brats.' Why, they are the most well behaved girls I've ever met."

Sadie snorted rudely and waved her hands in the air. All the other women looked up and then went back to their work, pretending not to notice her outburst. "You're just saying that because you're in love with him," she said in a voice that was rather too loud. "Well, you're *wilkom* to him! Things were going along just fine between us, until you showed up with your do-gooder ways, and got Simon to fall in love with you again."

Sadie stormed out of the *haus*, leaving Patience red faced and embarrassed. A few women smiled at her in support, but Patience ducked her head and got back to her work. Simon, in love with her? Well, that was just the assumption of an upset woman, but could it be true? She thought he had loved her once, before he had married Waneta. Yet could it be at all possible that he was in love with her now?

And, more to the point, how did Patience feel about Simon? She had never stopped loving him, despite everything he had done to her, but would she be able to put that in the past and move on?

CHAPTER 17

Patience was driving Blessing back from her *vadder's* buggy shop when he suddenly reared up. Patience at once looked around to see what had startled him, but couldn't see anything. "Whoa, steady, Blessing," she said in a soothing voice.

Blessing took one more step, and then cantered away. It wasn't as if he was bolting, galloping in a blind panic; it was just that he was cantering steadily, but there was nothing that Patience could do to stop him, turn him, or control him in any way.

Finally, Blessing came to a stop outside the bishop's *haus*. The bishop, Mr. Beiler, and his *fraa*, Linda, were standing outside their *haus*, and they looked shocked to see Blessing cantering up to them.

The bishop hurried over to Patience. "Is it your *vadder*?" he asked with concern in his voice.

Patience shook her head. "*Nee*, he's fine. Blessing suddenly took off and brought me here. I couldn't stop him."

The bishop's *fraa* chuckled, and the bishop looked amused. "That horse has quite the reputation," he said, stroking his long, ginger *baard* which was graying. "I do believe that horse listens to *Gott* more than some people do. Well, it's obvious you need to talk to me. Come inside then."

Patience made to protest, but then changed her mind. Perhaps she did need to talk to the bishop after all. "I'll just tie up Blessing first."

"I'll see to him," the bishop's *fraa* said.

"He can undo knots," Patience warned her.

"He won't undo them today, now that he's brought you to see me," the bishop said.

Patience raised her eyebrows, thinking that it was a strange thing for the bishop to say. The bishop looked stern, with his long, narrow face, and long, pointed nose, but Patience remembered him as being kind and understanding. He was distantly related to her *vadder*, and had the same caring manner.

The bishop indicated that Patience sit down in the low, adirondack chair opposite him. As Patience sank into the deeply upholstered seat, she wondered why an adirondack chair would be inside; surely it was outdoor furniture.

Patience looked up at the bishop, who was sitting at a much higher level than she was, in a high back, four poster, swivel glider.

Before Patience had time to speak, the bishop's wife, Linda, hurried into the room. She set down a tray, on top of which were two large mugs of hot, meadow tea, on the little, round table between them. "I'll just fetch you both the shoo fly pie."

Patience chewed anxiously on a fingernail while she waited for Linda Beiler to return. Thankfully it appeared that the bishop wasn't going to push her to speak. Soon, Patience had a plate, a fork, and slice of wet bottom shoo fly pie on her lap.

"So," the bishop finally said, "what would you like to talk to me about?"

Patience thought before answering. It was her borrowed horse, Blessing, that had brought her to the bishop's *haus*. She herself had no plans of visiting the bishop at all, but she thought that might be rude if she pointed that out. Patience shrugged. Well, she was here, so she might as well tell the bishop everything.

"It's little embarrassing," she said.

"Well, just take your time, and tell me all about it," the bishop said, smiling kindly.

Patience set her plate down on the table and tried to stop her knees shaking. She pushed her heels firmly into the ground, and that had the desired effect of preventing her knees knocking together. "As you know," she began, "I was engaged to Simon Warner some years ago." She looked up the bishop, who simply nodded, so she continued. "As you know," she repeated, I went to live with my *Aenti* Carrie in Ohio after I wrecked the truck when I was on *rumspringa*."

"And why did you do that?" the bishop asked.

Patience shifted uncomfortably under the bishop's gaze. "I was on vacation with my *familye* in Florida, and we came back early. I went looking for Simon and saw Waneta and Simon together in a café. Later that day, Waneta told me that she and Simon had started dating when I was on vacation, and that they were getting married. I was so upset that I drove away, hit the utility pole, and ended up in the hospital."

Patience looked at the bishop for a reaction, but he was finishing his shoo fly pie. She took a deep breath and continued. "I've never stopped loving Simon, but I'm having trouble forgiving him for what he did to me. I was heartbroken all those years ago, and the whole thing caused me to live away in Ohio for the last six years."

The bishop set down his plate and his fork. "Has Simon forgiven you?'

Patience was taken aback, and clutched at her throat. "Me? Whatever did I do? Simon was the one who did something wrong."

"What did he do, exactly?" the bishop asked.

Patience frowned. The bishop was not making any sense whatsoever. She had just told him what Simon had done, and, at any rate, the whole community knew that he had married Waneta.

She stared at the bishop, but when he made no move to speak, Patience thought she had better break the silence. "I was engaged to Simon. I went on vacation. When I got back, I saw Simon and Waneta laughing together. Later that day, Waneta told me that she and Simon had been dating behind my back and were getting married." Patience had no idea how to explain it in any simpler terms than that.

The bishop tapped his chin with one finger. "And you believed her?"

Patience went cold all over. It seemed to her that the room was spinning. She was suddenly afraid she would faint. "What do you mean?" she stammered.

"You believed Waneta?'

Patience stared at the bishop. "Well, *jah*. She was my friend."

The bishop nodded. "But Simon, he was your friend also, surely?"

Patience frowned. "But Waneta was my friend, and she's Amish."

The bishop raised his bushy eyebrows. "If you are saying that Amish don't lie, I will sadly have to point out to you the facts of the matter. Someone lied to you. It was either Waneta, or it was Simon. Yet it seems to me, that you believed Waneta and not Simon. Why was that?"

Patience reached for her hot meadow tea and took a large sip. Her mouth had run dry. "Why would Waneta lie to me?"

"Why indeed."

Patience stared in horror at the bishop. "Are you trying to tell me that Waneta lied to me? That I had all those injuries because of Waneta? That Simon and I broke up because Waneta lied to me?"

"More to the point," the bishop said, "you could not prevent Waneta lying to you. But you chose to believe her. You chose not to believe your betrothed, Simon. You chose to drive away too fast, and you chose to live in Ohio without first ascertaining the facts of the matter."

Patience sat there with her mouth hanging open.

"What do you think the Scriptures are for?" the bishop asked. Without waiting for Patience to answer, he continued. "Second Timothy chapter three, verses sixteen and seventeen tell us, '*All scripture is given by inspiration of God, and is profitable for doctrine, for reproof, for correction, for instruction in righteousness: That the man of God may be perfect, thoroughly furnished unto all good works."*

He gave Patience a searching look, and then continued. "We can't go wrong if we follow the Scriptures. They are there to guide us in the way we should go. And what did the Scriptures tell you to do in that situation?'

"Err, um," was all Patience could say.

The bishop continued. "The Scriptures told you to take your concerns to David, face to face. Matthew chapter eighteen, verses fifteen through seventeen:

'If your brother sins against you, go and tell him his fault, between you and him alone. If he listens to you, you have gained your brother.

But if he does not listen, take one or two others along with you, that every charge may be established by the evidence of two or three witnesses.

If he refuses to listen to them, tell it to the church.'"

Patience was horror stricken. Why hadn't she ever considered that Waneta had lied to her? Why had she accepted what Waneta had said at face value? And if she had followed what the Scriptures set down, she would have confronted Simon, and found out whether or not Waneta was lying. How could she have been so foolish?

Patience tried to stop bursting into tears. She took a few deep breaths and then another sip of hot meadow tea to try to calm herself. "How could I have been so foolish?" she finally asked the bishop.

"You were young," he said kindly, "and you did have rather a severe concussion, which might have contributed to your choices afterwards, if not before. Nevertheless, we cannot change the past; we can only change the future. The first two verses of the book of Hebrews, chapter twelve, say, *"Let us also lay aside every weight, and sin which clings so closely, and let us run with endurance the race that is set before us, looking to Jesus, the founder and perfecter of our faith, who for the joy that was set before him endured the cross, despising the shame, and is seated at the right hand of the throne of God."*

Patience rubbed her forehead. "So you are saying that I should not be concerned by my past mistakes, but that instead I should keep my eyes on Jesus and keep pressing forward, trying to be guided by the Scriptures from now on?"

The bishop nodded.

CHAPTER 18

"Blessing, Blessing!" Patience had called and called, but there was still no sign of her borrowed horse. She had gone out to hitch Blessing to the buggy, but he was not in his stall. Patience followed some hoof prints, but she had no idea whether they were fresh ones or not. The hoof prints led her to the iced over pond.

Patience gave a start as Simon hurried up behind her. "Is that you calling out, Patience?"

"*Jah*, it's me. I'm looking for my horse,

Blessing." *I'm not calling out for Gott to bless me*, she wanted to add, but figured that Simon might not find that funny.

"How did he get away?" Simon asked, walking toward her.

Patience threw her hands in the air. "He has a habit of letting himself out, but I tied the latch to the stall door with an extra piece of rope and knotted it double. I guess he just gets his teeth in and wiggles things loose."

Simon gave a low chuckle. "Horses have got a mind of their own sometimes."

"This one more than any other I've ever known," Patience said, hoping that Blessing was just quietly grazing somewhere.

Simon smiled. "Look behind you."

Patience saw Blessing walking toward her. "Blessing, naughty boy, come here." Patience slipped the headstall in her hand over his head.

Simon stroked Blessing's glossy neck. "Stay and talk for a while, that is, if you're not on your way somewhere."

"I can talk for a while. Do you have something in particular you want to speak about?" *Like why you married Waneta?* Patience thought.

Simon looked handsome, and the wind had brushed his hair around his face. "I don't know any other way to say this, Patience, other than to come straight out and say it. I've never been one to say fancy things."

Patience frowned and wondered if she had done something to gain his disapproval.

"The thing is, Patience, that I've fallen in love with you. More accurately, I've always been in love with you, and try as I might, I can't shake the love in my heart that I've always had for you."

Patience's mouth dropped open—she didn't know what to say. If this was true, why did he marry another woman? She knew that he was not someone who would tell a lie, not now anyway, and she still did not know whether it had been Simon or Waneta who had been lying all those years ago.

Simon seemed uncomfortable with her silence. "If you don't feel the same way any more, maybe you might grow to love me too. I think I would make a *gut* husband, and you love the girls, that's plain to see."

Patience rubbed her forehead. "Have you loved me since we were young?"

Simon nodded. "I've loved you forever, since... well, I can't remember when I started, but I don't remember ever not loving you."

Patience felt a throbbing in her temples. "Why did you marry Waneta if you loved me?"

Simon's face went white. "You left the community, Patience. I thought I'd never see you again. You seemed so angry with me when you were in the hospital, and I had no idea why."

Patience trembled. "That's why I left, though, Simon. I only left because you were going to marry Waneta. I couldn't stay and see that happen."

Simon took a step closer to Patience. "But I only had any thought of marrying Waneta after you left."

Patience caught her breath. *Now*, she thought, *now I will find out once and for all if Waneta was lying*. "Simon, the day I came back from vacation early, I saw Waneta, and she told me that you and she had been dating while I was away and that the two of you were engaged."

Simon gasped. "Patience, that's not true, not true at all. Is that why you told me to go away when you were in the hospital, because you believed Waneta?"

Patience felt the tears threatening to fall and

tried to blink them away. So Simon had been telling the truth after all. "*Ach*, Simon, I'm so sorry. Can you ever forgive me? Waneta was so convincing. I believed her when she said that the two of you had started dating just before my *familye* and I went to Florida on vacation. I'm so sorry, Simon." Patience shook her head. What a fool she had been.

Simon looked down at his feet. "So that's what you've thought all these years?"

"*Jah.*" Patience could barely get out the one word. She felt utterly miserable.

Simon took off his hat and scratched his head. "I suppose I can tell you the full truth of the matter now, since Waneta is no longer with us. After you left, Waneta tricked me into marrying her. She admitted it to me a few months later. Waneta told me that she had gotten herself into a compromising situation with an *Englischer* and that she was having a baby. She said that it had happened on her

rumspringa. She said that the *Englischer*
deserted her. With you gone, and thus my one
and only hope of love gone, I did the
honorable thing and saved her and her *familye*
from shame and married her. When no *boppli*
came, she said she'd had a miscarriage. I
challenged her on it, and she admitted that
she'd tricked me. She even laughed about it."

"*Ach*, Simon, I'm so sorry." Patience was
remorseful. If only she had gone to Simon and
set before him what Waneta had told her,
then the truth would have come to light back
then.

"I told her before I married her that I was in
love with you and I told her that I always
would be," Simon said. "She said she didn't
mind."

Patience gasped and covered her mouth.

Simon looked at the ground once more. "I did
everything I could to make the marriage work.
I thought that when the *kinner* came along

that would turn her into a different person, but she remained the same."

"I've always loved you, too," Patience blurted out.

Simon immediately looked up from the ground and into Patience's tear-filled eyes. "You've loved me too? You still love me even after all that's happened?"

Patience nodded. "Simon, I'm so, so sorry I messed things up for us by believing Waneta's lies all those years ago."

Simon stepped closer to her and wrapped his arms around her tightly.

Patience buried her head into his shoulder. "But if I hadn't done so you wouldn't have your two little miracles, Sarah and Katie. It's all in *Gott's* will, Simon. He knows best."

Simon took a step back from Patience and looked longingly into her eyes. "Will you marry me, Patience?"

Tears streamed down Patience's face. "I will, Simon. Of course I will."

Simon pulled her into his hard, muscled chest, and Patience felt she could stay there forever, safe and protected. With Simon's two little girls, their *familye* had a *gut* head start and Patience hoped if it were *Gott's* will that they would have many *kinner* together.

NEXT BOOK IN THIS SERIES

Kindness

Lydia is thirty years old, past the usual Amish age for marrying. She is convinced that no man will want her as she is overweight. In her attempts to remain invisible, Lydia's only outing is the church meeting every other week.

What happens when the handsome Eli Schrock arrives in her community and makes an instant impression on all the girls of marriageable age?

Lydia is also drawn to Eli Schrock, despite thinking that a man would never find her suitable. Tongues in the community start to wag when Eli Schrock goes out of his way to spend time with Lydia.

Will Lydia lower her barriers in time to allow Eli to see the true woman that she is, or will Eli's attention be drawn away to the more outgoing, confident girls in the community?

ABOUT RUTH HARTZLER

USA Today best-selling author, Ruth Hartzler, was a college professor of Biblical history and ancient languages. Now she writes faith-based romances, cozy mysteries, and archeological adventures.

Ruth Hartzler is best known for her Amish romances, which were inspired by her Anabaptist upbringing. When Ruth is not writing, she spends her time walking her dog and baking cakes for her adult children, all of whom have food allergies. Ruth also enjoys correcting grammar on shop signs when nobody is looking.

www.ruthhartzler.com

Made in the USA
Monee, IL
28 August 2021